This book belongs to:

....

....

Bright Sparks books have been especially created
in line with the **National Curriculum** and the
National Literacy and Numeracy Strategies.
They are designed to help young children achieve
success in their early learning years.

Retold by Monica Hughes
Illustrated by Gaby Hansen

Reading consultants: Betty Root and Monica Hughes

Marks and Spencer p.l.c.
PO Box 3339
Chester, CH99 9QS
www.marksandspencer.com

ISBN 1-84461-570-7
Printed in China

First Readers

Sleeping Beauty

MARKS &
SPENCER

Helping your child to read

First Readers are closely linked to the National Curriculum. Their vocabulary has been carefully selected from the word lists recommended by the National Literacy Strategy.

Read the story

Read the story
to your child
a few times.

The good fairy waved her wand and said,
"The princess will not die.
She will prick her finger
on a spinning wheel and go to
sleep for one hundred years."

So the king said, "Take all the spinning wheels out of the castle."

16

Follow your finger

Run your finger under
the text as you read.
Your child will soon begin to
follow the words with you.

Look at the pictures

Talk about the pictures. They will help your child to understand the story.

"The princess will not die."

17

Have a go

Let your child have a go at reading the large type on each right-hand page. It repeats a line from the story.

Join in

When your child is ready, encourage them to join in with the main story text. Shared reading is the first step to reading alone.

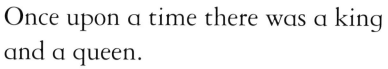

Once upon a time there was a king
and a queen.
The king and the queen had a baby.
The king said, "We can have a
party for the baby."
The queen said, "We can ask the
fairies to the party."

8

The king and the queen had
a baby.

The fairies came to the party.
The fairies came to see the baby.
The first fairy waved her wand.
"The princess will be happy," she said.
Then the other fairies waved their
wands.

The fairies came to see
the baby.

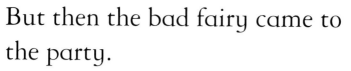

But then the bad fairy came to
the party.
She came to see the baby too.
She waved her wand and said,
"The princess will die."

"The princess will die."

The king and queen were sad.
They did not want the princess to die.
Then the good fairy came to
see the baby.

The king and queen were sad.

The good fairy waved her
wand and said,
"The princess will not die.
She will prick her finger
on a spinning wheel and go to
sleep for one hundred years."

So the king said, "Take all the spinning
wheels out of the castle."

"The princess will not die."

One day the princess was playing in
the castle.
She saw a little room at the top of
the castle.
The princess went into the room.

The princess went into
the room.

There was a spinning wheel in
the room.
The princess went to see it.
She pricked her finger on the spinning
wheel.
Then the princess went to sleep.
The king and the queen went to sleep.
Everyone in the castle went to sleep.

The princess went to sleep.

Everyone went to sleep for one
hundred years.
Thorns grew all over the castle.

One day a prince came by.
He saw the thorns all over the castle.
He cut down the thorns.
Then he went into the castle.
The prince saw everyone was asleep.

One day a prince came by.

The prince went into the little room at
the top of the castle.

The prince saw the princess.

When he saw the princess he fell in
love with her.

He kissed the princess and she
woke up.

Everyone in the castle woke up.

The prince saw the princess.

When the princess saw the prince she fell in love with him.
The princess was happy.
The prince was happy.
Everyone was happy.
And the prince and the princess lived happily ever after.

The prince and the princess
lived happily ever after.

Look back in your book.
Can you read these words?

king

queen

fairy

prince

baby

castle

Can you answer these questions?

What did the
bad fairy say?

Why does everyone in
the castle go to sleep?

How does
the princess
wake up?

First Readers
(subject to availability)

Chicken Licken
Cinderella
The Elves and the Shoemaker
The Enormous Turnip
The Gingerbread Man
Goldilocks and the Three Bears
Hansel and Gretel
Jack and the Beanstalk
Little Red Riding Hood
Snow White and the Seven Dwarfs
Sleeping Beauty
The Three Billy Goats Gruff
The Three Little Pigs
The Ugly Duckling

Look out for other books
in the **Bright Sparks** range:

**First Readers Book and CD sets
First Readers Sticker Books
Bright Sparks Workbooks
Bright Sparks Word Cards**